EARTH VERSES
and
WATER RHYMES

EARTH VERSES
and
WATER RHYMES

J. Patrick Lewis

illustrated by Robert Sabuda

ATHENEUM   1991   NEW YORK

Collier Macmillan Canada • Toronto
Maxwell Macmillan International Publishing Group
New York • Oxford • Singapore • Sydney

To Lida, Rita, and Kostia—
с любовью и уважением
                        —JPL

For my brother and sister,
Bruce and Wendy
                        —RS

Atheneum. Macmillan Publishing Company.
866 Third Avenue, New York, NY 10022
Collier Macmillan Canada, Inc., 1200 Eglinton Avenue East. Suite 200
Don Mills, Ontario M3C 3N1   First Edition
Printed in Hong Kong by South China Printing Company (1988) Ltd.
1 2 3 4 5 6 7 8 9 10

Library of Congress Cataloging-in-Publication Data. Lewis, J. Patrick.
Earth verses and water rhymes/by J. Patrick Lewis; illustrated
by Robert Sabuda.—1st ed. P.   cm.
Summary: A collection of poems celebrating the natural world
around us. ISBN 0-689-31693-3
1. Nature—Juvenile poetry.   2. Children's poetry, American.
[1. Nature—Poetry.   2. American poetry.]   I. Sabuda, Robert, ill.
II. Title. PS3562.E9465E27   1991 811′.54—dc20 90-40709 CIP AC

The art for this book was created from handcut linoleum prints.
Each block was inked and printed separately by hand.

Contents

Sounds of Winter

The Old October Ogres come
Without a fee-fi-fo or fum:
They lumber in *tum-tum-ti-tum.*

Nesting in trees forty feet tall,
They shake the leaves that fall in fall—
You hardly notice them at all.

But soon you hear the muffled snores
Of Dark December Dinosaurs,
Who wake to make the wind that roars,

The frost that bites, the ice that numbs,
The fee-fi-foes and dreadful fums…
When Ogres go and winter comes.

A Charm for the Trees

Juniper, hickory, walnut, fig
Make a wish on a twisted twig

Maple, apple, Colorado spruce
Syrup, cider, Christmas goose

Sycamore, cinnamon, buckeye, beech
Earth's umbrellas bloom out of reach

Snowflake

One winter day,
  five miles above
    my house, it dropped
    out of a cloud,
     swirling round
    a milky sky—
    slow fast slow—
not knowing where
  to go.

I waited and waited.
  Knew it would come.
  Tiny white button
  dizzied down,
   almost touched
  the ground. But
  suddenly it flew
back up and hung
one inch above
  my tongue.

The Red Fox

Have you heard her yipping
when the moon is down?

Have you seen her skipping
on the snow-coat hills?

The red fox dipping
her paintbrush paws
into the drifts she loves.

Fog

The
bone-
deep
chill
of
early
fall

when
night
slips
in-
to
her
white
silk
shawl

Spring Rain

I puddle up the neighborhood
    I make the mailman mad
I wake the worm and spank the frog
    Sleeping on his lily pad

And when the tulips in their beds
    Nod happily, it's true,
I shake the petals of their hands
    And say, How do you dew?

The White Wind

On Sunday there was a Wind
    dressed all in white—
    white coat and handkerchief and tie.

On Monday it rapped, rapped hard
    at the back door.

On Tuesday music jangled in the chimes.

On Wednesday something rocked the boats
    out on the bay.

On Thursday it hung over Charlotte's Hill.

On Friday Aunt Babe and gray clouds
    spent the afternoon.

On Saturday I took a nap and missed
    the White Wind. It dropped two rose
    petals on the porch. It left its tears
    on the windowpane.

Lighthouse

This giant white
  Land candle burns
The edges of
  The fog by turns.

The lonely keeper
  Of the flame
Illuminates
  One picture frame—

A ship returning
  Welcome light
And slipping safely
  Through the night.

Ocean

Grandest of canyons
Home to gray whales
Oodles of islands
Dotted with sails

Upside-down mountain
Atlantic lagoon
Pacific horizon
Mirror to the moon

Stage for a sunset
Rainbow's end
Iceberg deep freezer
The dolphin's friend

Who wants to muffle
The ocean's roar
That's what a mighty
Blue ocean's for

Sand House

I built a house
   One afternoon
With bucket, cup
   And tablespoon,

Then scooped a shovel-
   ful of shore
On top to add
   The second floor.

But when the fingers
   Of the sea
Reached up and waved
   A wave to me,

It tumbled down
   Like dominoes
And disappeared
   Between my toes.

Honeycomb Days

**Brown sugar nights
Honeycomb days
Cinnamon afternoons**

**Hot weather stirs
This blue bowl of sky
Sweet spoonfuls
Of July**

Puppy

Summer is a long yellow gown
Fitted to the fields and farms.

Buttoned to a blue-necked sky,
It flutters its empty arms

Over the trees. The farm boy
Calls to the little nutbrown

Puppy tugging at the hem
Of summer's evening gown.

Dance of the Mushrooms

Mushrooms tipping their caps—
   this is all you ever see.

      But when night falls
         through the trees,
      and no one is watching,
         they brown shyly
         and begin to dance.

            Bowing softly,
         they waltz in the dark
         to the wind's guitar.
         But when light falls
         through the trees,

mushrooms tipping their caps—
   this is all you ever see.

Grasshopper

Silence

       stilled the meadow

   as if

      the cricket din

had stopped

     to hear

   the solo

       of

      the first

       violin

Blue Herons

One swoops in on a glider wing
Two stick-picks the shore

Three stands stiff as a soldier boy
Waiting for soldier four

Five parades in his downy coat
Six inspects a toad

Seven leans into a singing wind
Eight's on the river road

Nine flies up to the bird-bent tree
Ten wears a midnight plume

Eleven talks back to the gossip wren
Twelve's in his watery room

Indian Summer

Blue brushes paint
   The afternoon.
My dog mistakes
   This heat for June.

The cornstalks, bent
   Like ragged men,
Wind-whisper *home*
   come home again.

Hay bales parade
   A country mile,
And winter waits
   A little while.

Then, getting on
   Towards evening,
My Grandpa creaks
   The glider swing

And tells me how
   It used to be
When *he* sat up
   On Grandpa's knee.

The World is Much

The world is much too full of cat,
Who think they own the place, and that

Is why the world's so full of bird,
Who sing this song you may have heard:

"Wherever you go, wherever you're at—
The world is much too full of cat!"

32